ZARA'S RULES

for LIVING YOUR

BEST LIFE

ZARA'S RULES
for LIVING YOUR
BEST LIFE

HENA KHAN

Illustrated by Wastana Haikal

SALAAM
READS

NEW YORK | LONDON | TORONTO
SYDNEY | NEW DELHI

SALAAM
R E A D S

An imprint of Simon & Schuster Children's Publishing Division
1230 Avenue of the Americas, New York, New York 10020

For information about special discounts for bulk purchases, please contact Simon & Schuster Special
Sales at 1-866-506-1949 or business@simonandschuster.com.
The Simon & Schuster Speakers Bureau can bring authors to your live event.
For more information or to book an event, contact the Simon & Schuster Speakers Bureau
at 1-866-248-3049 or visit our website at www.simonspeakers.com.
Also available in a Salaam Reads paperback edition
Interior design by Tom Daly
The text for this book was set in Adobe Caslon Pro.
The illustrations for this book were rendered digitally.
Manufactured in the United States of America
0223 FFG
First Salaam Reads hardcover edition March 2023
2 4 6 8 10 9 7 5 3 1
CIP data for this book is available from the Library of Congress.
ISBN 9781534497658 (hardcover)
ISBN 9781534497641 (paperback)
ISBN 9781534497665 (ebook)

To my inspiring young friend, Zara

ZARA'S
RULES
for
LIVING
YOUR
BEST
LIFE

Chapter 1

* ✳ *

"How about a marble roller coaster?" Naomi suggests from her stool, where she's swinging her legs back and forth.

"Yes!" Zayd cheers, before suddenly frowning and adding, "Wait. What's that?"

We can't help but laugh at my little brother, who has snuck into our clubhouse to listen to our conversation. Again.

"It's a roller coaster for a marble," Naomi explains. "You use stuff like foam and cardboard and make loops and hills to see how far you can get the marble to go."

I ponder this as I bite into a sugar cookie, one of the snacks Naomi brought for us today. A marble roller coaster sounds less exciting than a real one. But it could still be fun to make. And if it turns out well, we could add it to the Brisk River Book of Neighborhood Records under "Most Amazing Marble Roller Coaster."

"Let's add it to the list," I say.

Our list of "Things To Do Over Spring Break" is getting long already. Yesterday Jade added weaving friendship bracelets out of recycled plastic. Gloria wants to make homemade paletas, frozen fruity treats that she insists are better than flavored ice sticks. Alan said he's going to organize an "epic" Easter egg hunt. That gave Jade the idea to add decorating eggs to the list. And since Zayd is still deciding what he wants us all to do together over break, I left the space for number five blank for him. Melvin is traveling to Korea over break, so his ideas for things to do aren't on the list. And although Naomi's brother, Michael, hasn't come up with any suggestions yet, I know he'll have something to say about everything we do. He's in eighth grade already and has *lots* of opinions.

I write "marble roller coaster" on the whiteboard and stand back to admire the list. There's no way this isn't going to be the best spring break ever. None of the kids on our street can complain that we aren't doing something that they want. We've included everyone, which is the number one neighborhood rule for having fun. And all the activities sound like they could be a good—and even delicious—time.

"What supplies do we need?" Naomi asks. "Let's make sure we get everything ahead of time. We don't want another piñata situation."

I groan. Last summer we made a huge batch of glue mixture to craft a homemade piñata shaped like a strawberry. We followed step-by-step instructions from a video on YouTube. But since we didn't have any balloons, we used an old beach ball and layered the newspaper, glue, and tissue on top of it. It looked seriously amazing when we were finished. You're supposed to pop the balloon and take it out of the piñata when the glue is dry, and then you can put the candy inside. But the beach ball wouldn't pop no matter what we did, so we couldn't get to that step. Michael ended up shaking the bag of candy out around the yard instead. The candy flew everywhere, and everyone dove onto the grass and fought each other for it. Months later Melvin found a mini Tootsie Pop over by his garage.

"We'll get all the things we need!" I promise. "It's not that much. Except for maybe the roller coaster foam. And the eggs. And Popsicle sticks. But we still have a few days before break."

"I'll ask my mom if she can help us," Naomi offers.

I already know that Mrs. Goldstein is ready to help. She has an entire cabinet full of crafting supplies. It's like she's just waiting for us to ask her for pipe cleaners or tissue paper or googly eyes. My mom's answer when I ask her for stuff is usually "Check the garage," but you'd be surprised by all the useful things I've managed to dig out of there.

"Let's ask her now," Naomi says. "And I want to get a drink."

"Let's go, Zayd," I tell my brother. "Wipe up your crumbs, okay?"

The last thing we need is for Zayd to dirty up the clubhouse after we spent a whole hour spring cleaning it over the weekend. It's looking great now that we swept out all the dead leaves and grass, dusted it, and wiped down the stools. We've got the whiteboard and our book of records in there, along with tennis balls and jump ropes. After our stools and a tiny tray table for snacks, there's not much room for anything else. But it's still the perfect place to make plans, hide out, and take a break from the sun. And it was one of Naomi's best ideas ever to turn the old toolshed in her backyard into our fun-making headquarters.

"Hey, Mom?" Naomi asks as we head into her house and Zayd trots back across the street to our house. "Can you help us with supplies?"

"For what, honey?" Mrs. Goldstein asks. She's in the kitchen, chopping up herbs and throwing them into a bowl.

"For all the activities we planned for spring break,"

Naomi explains. "We need foam, Popsicle sticks, tape, and what else was there, Zara?"

"Oh dear." Mrs. Goldstein puts down her knife. "I thought I told you I signed you up for camp this break."

"What? You didn't tell me," Naomi says. "Which camp?"

We look at each other in surprise, and Naomi raises her eyebrows in a way that I know means, *I have no idea what's going on.*

"The temple is offering a day camp, so I signed you and Michael up," Mrs. Goldstein explains.

"Do I have to go?" Naomi pleads. "Zara and I already have the whole week planned out! We came up with a long list of things to do with everybody!"

"I've already paid for it," Mrs. Goldstein says, shaking her head as she wipes her hands on a dish towel. "So, yes, I'm afraid you do have to go. And besides, you'll like it. Your friends from Hebrew School will be there."

"Okay," Naomi says, even as her shoulders droop. "Come on, Zara."

Naomi grabs my hand, and we walk into the family room and sit down together on her sofa in stunned silence.

"Sorry," she finally whispers to me. "I had no idea."

"It's okay," I whisper back, even though my throat tightens as I speak. Spring break won't be the same without Naomi.

Chapter 2

* * *

Mama is scowling at the television while watching the news, so I wait for a commercial before asking my question.

"Can I go to Har Shalom's spring break camp?"

"Where?" Mama replies, turning her full attention to me.

"Naomi's going, and we had so many things we planned to do over break, so I thought maybe I'll just go to camp with her instead, because she said that it's really great and that it has all this—"

"Slow down." Mama holds up her hands like she does when she wants me to take a breath and stop speaking.

I pause.

"You want to go to camp at the . . . *synagogue?*" Mama asks.

"Yeah. With Naomi. I mean, I know it's probably mostly for Jewish kids. But remember when you said Muslims are so much like Jewish people when we were at Michael's bar mitzvah?"

"Yes, I remember," Mama says.

"So, then, it'll be okay for me to go, right?" I continue.

Mama makes a sound that's half cough, half laugh. "Listen, I'm sure the folks at Har Shalom would welcome you at the camp. But I already made plans for break," she finally says.

"You did?" I ask. Mama didn't tell me about any plans. That must be because it's a surprise. Maybe we're going on a trip! We've been talking about driving to the beach for a while. That's got to be it!

My mother pats the seat next to her, like she does

whenever she has big news. I begin to make a mental list of the items I'm going to pack for the beach. I can't forget to bring my new hat with the tiny pineapples all over it, and my swimming shoes if I can find them. I should probably make up some games for the car ride, so Zayd doesn't annoy us the whole time.

"I'm going to be tied up with a training at the office, and your father is extra busy with a proposal. So I thought you and Zayd could spend the week with Naano and Nana Abu," Mama continues.

Hold on. *What?*

"Does that mean we're not going to the beach?" I ask.

"No, Zara." Mama sighs. "Not the beach. You two are on spring break, but Baba and I still have work. Don't worry, your grandparents are excited to take care of you two and spend the week with you. Especially now that Nana Abu is retired and has more free time, remember?"

She says it like I could have already forgotten the special dinner to celebrate Nana Abu's retirement last week. Even though it was a party, it seemed to make him happy and sad at the same time. He worked at the same company for thirty-seven years, and now he won't be going there or seeing his co-workers anymore.

"It would be better to go on a vacation," I say.

Zayd, who somehow always appears whenever there's big news, rushes into the room.

"Where are we going?" he asks, breathless.

"Not to the beach," I mutter.

"You're going to Naano's house, for spring break," Mama tells him.

Zayd's eyes grow wide. "For the whole week? Are we sleeping there? Are you and Baba coming too?" he asks.

"No, Zayd. Just you and Zara during the day. I'll drop you off and pick you up, like we already do when they take care of you. You'll have a great time."

Zayd looks at me now, his eyes wider. "We have to be there for the whole entire break?" he squeaks.

"I know," I add. "Can't we stay at home?" I ask Mama. "That way we can at least still play with Gloria, Jade, and Alan. We have a whole long list of plans."

"I can't leave you alone all day." Mama shakes her head. "I won't be here, and Baba needs to go to meetings too."

"But I'm old enough," I argue. "People stay home alone at my age."

"Not until you're twelve." Mama is firm. "Come on, you two. You always have a good time whenever you go there. Naano makes you so many treats."

That part's true. Naano loves to feed us, especially Zayd, who she calls her "skinny mouse." She makes us her best Pakistani dishes, like kabobs with no onions or tomatoes, chicken biryani, and her famous parathas. Plus she secretly lets us have junk food like chips and cookies from packages that Mama doesn't like to buy. But Naano also has a list of chores for us to do for her whenever we visit. And she likes to watch her Pakistani dramas turned up super loud, yell into the phone to relatives in Pakistan, and spend a long time praying. Honestly, it gets pretty boring after a few hours.

Like she's reading my mind, Mama speaks up again. "I've already talked to Naano, and she says she'll make sure you play games and do plenty of fun things. Think of it as ... Camp Naano." Mama smiles at her own joke, but Zayd and I don't smile back.

"Shouldn't we get to decide what we want to do for our own break?" I grumble. I mean, first Mrs. Goldstein signed Naomi up for Har Shalom camp without telling her, and now my mom's sending us to this so-called Naano camp without asking us, either.

"You can decide to have a good attitude and make the best of this," Mama says, turning her attention back to the news.

Zayd turns to me and shrugs. There's no changing Mama's mind.

"Besides, you can see your friends when you get home, and on the weekend," Mama adds.

"I guess," I say. But I already know that it isn't going to be the same.

Chapter 3

✳ ✳ ✳

Naano opens the door and then spreads open her arms for a hug. Zayd and I dive in, and she gives us a firm squeeze.

"Asalaamualaikum!" she says. "My smart girl and my skinny mouse are here."

"Remember to be good," Mama warns as she gives her mother a quick kiss and turns to leave.

"I'm always good," Naano says, and snorts.

"She means us!" Zayd giggles while Naano winks at me. People say that I have my grandmother's quickness and sense of humor. I can see that, although sometimes it's hard to tell whether Naano is joking or not. And everyone usually knows when I'm being funny.

"Don't tire out Naano and Nana Abu too much," Mama adds, handing me my backpack. It's filled with books, notepads, and markers that I brought to keep us busy, just in case.

"Me? Tired? I won't get tired. I'm a young chick," Naano replies.

Zayd smiles at me. Naano is in a playful mood. Maybe we were just overreacting and this is going to be a good week after all.

"Bye, Mama," we say as we slip off our shoes, leave them by the door, and head into the house.

Nana Abu is sitting in the family room, still wearing his fuzzy blue robe and slippers.

"What are you doing?" I ask after we greet him. It's strange to see our grandfather in his pajamas. He always dressed up extra nice when he went to work, and way nicer than the rest of us on the weekends. Nana Abu is someone who tucks his shirt into his jeans and wears a belt, and I've never seen him in shorts or sweatpants.

"Just waiting for you," Nana Abu says. "And watching the markets."

"What should we do?" I ask. "Do you want to maybe, you know, change your clothes, and then we can go to the park, or to Carmen's for ices and frozen custard, or maybe to the library?"

"Carmen's!" Zayd yells. "Raspberry gelati!"

"Maybe later." Nana Abu smiles. "Isn't it time for breakfast?"

"We were waiting to eat with you," Naano says. "Come on, the chai is ready."

Nana Abu gets up and shuffles into the kitchen, still in his pajamas, where Naano has spread out a gigantic breakfast feast. There's eggs and parathas and chanas and halwa.

"Yum!" Zayd's eyes light up when he sees the parathas, even though we already had oatmeal before coming over. He's one of the pickiest eaters on the planet, but Naano's parathas are something he never refuses. Sometimes, when he won't eat anything else on the table, Naano spreads butter and sugar on the flaky bread and rolls it up for him while my parents complain about how she's spoiling him. To be fair, it's too late. He's already spoiled.

Nana Abu helps himself to the halwa first. I'm certain that if Mama was here, she would complain that it's too much sugar and try to fill his plate with cucumbers instead.

"This is the best part of retirement," Nana Abu says as he digs into his food. "Alhumdulilah, no more breakfast sandwiches and burnt coffee from the deli in my building."

"I love that deli," I say, remembering the time when Nana Abu took Zayd and me to pick up some papers from his office. He bought us chips and drinks, and the owners wouldn't stop gushing about how cute we were. They even let us pick out whatever candy we wanted for free. I got a ring pop that lit up. I'd be happy to go to work just to have a deli like that to go to every day.

I take a little bit of the sticky and sweet halwa and eat it with a bite of paratha. Yum!

"Milk?" Naano asks, pouring me a glass before I can answer her.

"I don't like milk," Zayd starts to complain, but I kick him under the table before we get a lecture on why we need to drink milk if we want to grow big and tall and strong.

"OW!" Zayd yells, extra loudly. "Stop it!"

"Leave him," Naano scolds me. "What's wrong with you?"

"Can we go somewhere or do something now?" I ask, trying to change the subject. "Mama says this is going to be Camp Naano."

"I have to clean up first," Naano says, standing to take the empty chai cups to the sink. "You play with Nana Abu."

We follow Nana Abu as he shuffles back to the family room and settles onto the couch.

"Want to go outside?" Zayd asks him.

"In a little while," Nana Abu says. "I'm just going to rest for a bit first."

"From breakfast?" Zayd says. "But all you did was eat."

Nana Abu smiles and gently touches Zayd on the chin.

"You wait until you're my age, Zaydoo. I'm digesting," he says.

And then our grandfather puts his feet up on the ottoman, closes his eyes, and falls right asleep.

"What's he doing?" Zayd whispers to me. "Why is he sleeping in the morning? Didn't he just wake up?"

"Yeah," I whisper back. This is definitely strange behavior from our grandfather. We need to find out what is going on with him. Because there needs to be less napping and more activities for Camp Naano to have a chance at being any fun at all.

Chapter 4

* * *

"I'm bored," Zayd declares as we walk back into the kitchen. "Nana Abu's sleeping."

"Here. Dry this." Naano hands him a towel and a cup.

"I thought we were supposed to have fun here this week," Zayd argues. "Not do work. Remember?"

"Don't be butthameez," Naano scolds. "You can help your grandmother for some of the time too."

"Why is Nana Abu still in his pajamas and sleeping again?" I ask, quickly moving away before Naano gives me any dishes.

"Let him rest," Naano says. "He worked hard for many years, and now he's retired and wants to take a break."

I think about the only retired person I've ever known, our neighbor Mr. Chapman. Before he moved to Florida, when he was still living in Naomi's house, he was always busy doing something. He'd read on his porch, make fresh lemonade from scratch, paint on an easel, and play tennis with other retired people. Now that I think of it, he made retirement look so awesome, I couldn't wait until I was old enough to retire myself.

"Aren't retired people supposed to do stuff like play golf and have rose gardens?" I ask.

"I wish I could make your grandfather work in the garden. Did you see all those weeds in the back?" Naano shakes her head. "Why don't you and Zayd go pull them?"

"But I thought—" Zayd starts.

"Go, go, that's a good idea. I'll bring Nana Abu," Naano says, with a gentle push toward the back porch. "It's so nice outside. It will feel good."

"Come on, Zayd," I say with a sigh. "The sooner we get

the weeding done, the sooner we can do something fun."

"Mein tujay *fun* dekhaungi," Naano says as she shuffles over to where Nana Abu is snoozing. I don't speak Urdu, but I understand Naano well enough to figure out she's saying something like, "I'll show you fun."

Zayd follows me outside and starts to climb onto the patio furniture.

"Watch out! The ground is made out of lava!" he yells.

"We're supposed to be gardening, Zayd," I remind him. But he dives off a chair onto the grass, ignoring me.

A few minutes later Nana Abu shuffles outside, wearing crisply pressed pants and a collared shirt that is way too nice for yard work. But at least he looks like himself again.

He joins me, and we stand together and stare at the plants in the ground.

"Which ones are weeds?" I ask.

"The ones that curl like those." Nana Abu points at some of the green leaves creeping out of the mulch.

"Weeding is boring! Can we play kickball instead? Do you have a ball?" Zayd runs over to a plastic storage container and starts to rummage through it. He throws out a hose, a mini shovel, and a bunch of plastic containers.

TAP! TAP! TAP!

Naano is rapping on the window, and we hear a muffled yell. "Don't make mess, Zayd!"

Zayd picks up the mini shovel and starts to dig a hole that isn't anywhere near the weeds. "I found a worm!" he yells. He picks it up with his fingers and waves the squiggly pinkish brown worm in my direction.

"Gross, Zayd! Put it back," I say.

"I'm going to keep him as a pet. I'm putting him into that bucket," Zayd insists.

"Zayd!" Naano scolds as she comes outside with a big paper bag. "I said no mess. And no worms. Come help me."

She and Nana Abu start weeding, and I notice that it's kind of hard for my grandparents to bend down. They make groaning sounds as they yank the weeds out of the ground, and breathe heavily when they stand back up to drop them into the bag. No wonder she wants us to do it.

"We'll finish up the rest," I volunteer, even though Zayd hasn't picked a single weed yet.

"Are you sure?" Naano asks as she quickly drops herself onto a patio chair.

"Thank you," Nana Abu adds as he joins her. He takes off his hat and mops his brow with a neatly folded handkerchief. There's dirt on his nice pants.

"I found a slug now!" Zayd says. He crouches on the ground and pokes it with a stick.

"Leave it alone, Zayd," I repeat. "You'll hurt it!"

"It's so slimy!" he squeals. The slug is gray with white spots, like a snail with no shell. There's a trail of wetness underneath it.

"Why don't you give him a drink," Nana Abu suggests. "Slugs like water."

"Yes, and water the rest of the plants too after you're done with the weeds," Naano adds.

That sounds like a terrible idea to me, but Zayd doesn't waste any time running over to connect the hose to the faucet. He waters the weeds, the slug, and all the dirt on the patio, which quickly turns into mud. But our grandparents aren't watching anymore and have already shuffled back into the house, mumbling that it's too bright for them.

I let Zayd play in the water while I weed, and soon he's soaking wet.

"Water fight!" he yells, turning the hose on me.

"No fair!" I protest, since there's only one hose. But the cool spray actually feels good when it hits my arms.

When everything is totally drenched, including me, we turn off the hose. I play lava pit with Zayd until we dry off and he decides he's ready for a snack.

"What are we going to do now?" Zayd says to me as he pulls open the porch door. "Something else fun, right?"

He's soggy and there are bits of weeds and leaves in his hair, but he turns and looks at me with hope in his eyes. He still believes this is going to be like a real camp, with nonstop activities, even though I know better. It's clear that if I don't think of something quick, he's going to be completely miserable all week. And that'll make the rest of us miserable too.

Chapter 5

* ✻ *

"What are you doing?" Zayd asks me.

I'm sitting in Nana Abu's office with a pad of paper and a pencil, thinking hard after lunch.

"Working on something, Zayd."

"But I'm bored."

"That's what I'm trying to fix!"

"How? You're not playing with me, and you're just sitting there, which is boring." Zayd plops down onto the carpet and stares up at the ceiling.

"Go ask Naano for something to do," I suggest.

"No way. She wants me to organize the cans in the pantry. She told me it's like playing with heavy blocks."

That sounds like Naano. She'll never stop trying new ways to trick us into doing chores.

"I'm making a list of the things that kids do at camp. And then we can come up with a schedule for what to do each day for the rest of the week, so we're not bored anymore."

"What kind of things?" Zayd picks up his head and tries to peek over my shoulder.

"Like water games."

"We just did water."

"I know."

"What else?"

To be honest, I haven't been to camp before. All I know are things I've read about or seen on TV.

"Like doing archery, going boating, and toasting marshmallows on a campfire," I say.

"Where are we going to boat at Naano's house?" Zayd throws up his hands. "Or do archery?"

"Right. Well, we can play board games."

"Naano only likes Monopoly. And it takes so long. And she always wins," Zayd complains. It's true. Naano does always win. She doesn't like to trade properties, and somehow she's a wizard at rolling doubles.

"How about cards?" I ask.

"Okay. Come on, then. Let's go ask," Zayd sighs.

Naano is folding laundry in the living room, and when she sees us, she smiles.

"Can we play a game?" Zayd asks.

"Want to play a memory game?" she offers.

"Okay," I say.

"Take these socks and line them up—"

"Naano! You're trying to make us fold the socks!" Zayd accuses.

Nana Abu looks up from his book and chuckles.

"Well, it can be fun," Naano says. She takes a balled-up pair of socks and throws it at Zayd.

"Laundry fight!" Zayd yells. He grabs an undershirt from the basket and flings it toward me. A pair of Nana

Abu's boxers are stuck to them and float to the floor near his foot. Zayd picks them up and puts them over his head and dances around.

"Okay, okay, bas kharo," Naano laughs. "I'm not washing these again."

"Can we play a real game?" I ask.

"Monopoly?" Naano brightens.

"How about cards?" I suggest.

"But Monopoly is better," Naano says. "There's money and hotels—"

"Mama will be here soon to pick us up," Zayd interrupts. "It takes so long. And that's boring."

"Boring shmoring," Naano grumbles. "Fine. Go get the cards from the drawer."

Zayd and I take turns playing War with Naano first, and then she teaches us a game that she used to play in Pakistan called "Rung." We convince Nana Abu to join us since the game needs four people, and we sit around the dining table. It's Naano and me versus Zayd and Nana Abu.

"Nana Abu! That was rung." Zayd slaps his own head when our grandfather makes a mistake and throws down the wrong card.

"Oh ho, I forgot," Nana Abu says. But then he tosses down another card he should have played earlier.

Zayd doesn't quite get the strategy either, so the two of them keep losing, and he starts complaining. Naano and I are winning so easily that I don't need her to give me sneaky signals to try to let me know which cards to throw, but she does it anyway. She moves her eyebrows up and down and flicks her pinky finger at me. I have absolutely no idea what she's trying to tell me to do, though, so it probably doesn't count as cheating.

We're arguing over whose turn it is to deal when Mama appears. No one hears the door open, or her come in, so she startles us.

"Aww, this is nice," Mama says, beaming. "I'm glad you're having a good time."

"Are you hungry?" Naano asks. "Want some chai?"

Mama nods. "Sure, I could go for some—"

"Bye!" Zayd doesn't wait for our mother to finish her sentence. He hugs both our grandparents, runs to the door, and starts to put on his shoes.

Mama laughs. "I guess someone is in a hurry to get home," she says.

"Kyunh, Zayd?" Naano asks. "You didn't have fun today?"

Zayd glances at me first, and then answers our grandmother in his super-honest seven-year-old way. "It was a little fun. But also kind of boring."

I feel my face heat up, embarrassed for Naano and Nana Abu. But they don't seem to mind at all.

"Allah Hafiz," they say cheerfully as they shuffle to the door to wave goodbye. And as we walk down the steps, I hear Nana Abu ask Naano for the remote.

Chapter 6

* ✱ *

On the drive home Mama asks us all about our day, like what we did and everything we ate. Zayd fills her in but spends most of the time describing every single detail imaginable about the slug.

"You okay, Zara?" Mama asks as we pull into our driveway. She turns around to face me. "You've been quiet."

"Yeah." I don't want to complain to Mama, especially after she mentioned how long and tiring her training was today. But I'm still thinking about how I'm going to get through a whole week of Camp Naano *and* keep Zayd entertained, if it's going to be like today. Plus, seeing Nana Abu in his pajamas and sleeping during the day sits like a weight on my chest.

We're barely out of the car when Naomi runs over from across the street.

"Hey, Zara!" she says, smiling brightly. "Can you play?"

"Can I?" I ask my mom.

"Sure, until dinner," Mama says. "How was your first day of camp, Naomi?"

"So awesome! The counselors are really nice. We're getting ready for Passover next week, so we made afikomen bags and decorated them."

"What's that?" I ask.

"At the end of the seder, we all search for a hidden piece of matzah that's in the bag."

I've tasted matzah before and like it. I make a mental note to add "holiday crafts" to my list of camp activities.

"Sounds nice," Mama says as she walks into the house. "Come on, Zayd. You need to hit the shower first. And then you, Zara, when you come in."

Naomi reaches into her pocket and then holds out her hand.

"This is for you," she says. There's a colorful string-shaped thing on her palm, curled up like the worm Zayd found earlier.

"Oh, thanks," I say, taking it gingerly. "What is it?"

"A friendship bracelet. I wasn't sure if we'd have time to make the ones Jade wanted us to do together over break, so I made these for us. See? I have one too!"

Naomi holds up her wrist, and I see her matching bracelet, which makes me feel instantly better. She ties mine on for me, and we walk over toward the clubhouse. But instead of going inside it, we flop down onto the grass

under the big tree in the Goldsteins' yard. The young leaves are bright green, and the sun is shining through them in a way that makes everything seem speckled.

"What else are you doing at your camp?" I ask Naomi, so that I can take notes.

"Tomorrow we're going to the Sandy Spring Adventure Park and doing the obstacle course and going zip-lining! I can't wait."

"Lucky!" I say. I've always wanted to go to the Adventure Park.

"I know. My friends and I are going to try to do the hardest level," Naomi says. She pauses and adds, "I wish you could come with us."

"Me too." I wonder if I can convince Naano and Nana Abu to take us. I imagine Naano zip-lining, and the thought makes me smile. But I can already hear her saying, "What is this zip-lining shmip-lining? Why can't you play here? Climb the tree in the yard. And then when you're done, you can lay down some mulch."

Naomi continues to gush about her amazing camp,

the hilarious counselor who likes to prank everyone, and everything else they've got planned for the rest of the week.

"We're making tie-dyed T-shirts and homemade ice cream," she says. "We're playing Capture the Flag and lots of different sports. And at the end of the week, there's a talent show! I'm going to juggle. I've been practicing a lot, and I'm getting better."

"What about your magic routine?" I remind her. Naomi's been working on her magic tricks and has gotten decent at a few of them.

"Oh yeah, I guess I could do that, too. But I want to try something different."

That's one of the things I love about Naomi. She's always trying out new hobbies, just like me. And even if I don't always stick with everything I do, that way I still manage to figure out what stuff I like best and what I can live without.

Which makes me realize something.

"That's it!" I suddenly sit up.

"What?" Naomi asks, looking puzzled.

"Nana Abu needs a hobby!"

"Your grandfather?"

"Yeah. He just started being retired. And I thought he'd act more like Mr. Chapman—the man who lived in this house before you."

"Right." Naomi nods slowly, like she's still trying to figure out what I'm talking about.

"Mr. Chapman did all these cool activities, and he was always making things. But my grandpa sat around and napped and watched TV most of the day today. Maybe he just needs hobbies. And I can help him find some!"

"Oh yeah, I'm sure you can do that," Naomi says. "You're amazing at having hobbies."

I'm sure too. I was literally born for this job.

"I'm going to make up my own camp, a real one, with a schedule of activities and everything," I add. "Because Camp Naano is basically a lot of eating and chores, even though she promised it would be fun. With my camp I can keep Zayd busy, so he's not bouncing off the walls, and I'm sure Nana Abu will find something new that he loves to do!"

42

"I can help you!" Naomi says.

We head to the clubhouse, and I use my notebook to make a list of all the different fun things we should be able to do at my grandparents' house. Then I come up with the "Rules for Camp Zara":

- Every day will include arts-and-crafts time, physical fitness time, and nature time.
- Everyone has to try new things until they find a hobby they like.
- I get to be the counselor.
- No complaining to the counselor, unless you're hurt.

By the time I go home to shower before dinner, I'm excited to go back to my grandparents' house tomorrow and start Camp Zara. Just like that, I've figured out how to fix everything.

Chapter 7

* * *

I roll the suitcase up the steps to the front after Mama drops us off at Naano's. When Naano opens the door, she points at my bag.

"Are you sleeping over here today?" she asks, making room for me to squeeze past her. "Your mother didn't tell me."

"No, no, we're still going home later. I just brought some more things for us to do."

"Oh, don't worry, I have so many things that you can do," Naano says. She points to the closet. "You can put together that new shoe rack for me. And upstairs I have some boxes that need—"

"I mean *fun* things, Naano," I interrupt. "Remember?"

"Okay, okay, fun things ki bachi," Naano says. "Come, I made you a fun thing for breakfast."

"French toast!" Zayd cheers from the kitchen after he kicks off his shoes and runs to the table. "Come on, Nana Abu! Let's eat."

Nana Abu puts down the newspaper and shuffles into the kitchen, wearing his robe and slippers again. He smiles at us and tousles Zayd's hair as he takes his seat.

Naano made potatoes with the French toast, and there's a bowl of cut-up fruit.

"This is so good," Zayd says as he stuffs a forkful of food into his face.

"Don't talk with your mouth full, Zayd," I remind him.

"You don't talk with *your* mouth full," he retorts.

"My mouth isn't full," I say, opening it extra wide before sticking my tongue out at him.

"Behave, you two," Naano commands.

"Are you done?" I ask my grandfather as he sips his chai. I'm ready to get started.

"Almost," Nana Abu says, and he drains the last of his cup. "Why?"

"I'll show you. Come on!" I get up from my seat and lead Nana Abu into the family room. He sits on the sofa while I unzip my suitcase and reveal what's inside. "Ta-da!"

"What's all this?" Nana Abu says.

"I thought it would be fun to have more organized activities at Camp Zara this week," I explain. Now that I'm calling it "Camp Zara" aloud, I really like the sound of it. "I'll be the counselor. It'll keep Zayd happy. And I thought it would be cool for you to find a new hobby, Nana Abu," I say, holding up a paintbrush.

"That's nice." Nana Abu pats my hand, and then settles into the sofa and picks up the newspaper.

"We're starting with craft time," I continue. "What do you want to do first? I have watercolors, and clay, and straw for making baskets. And I brought a bunch of old magazines if you want to make a collage."

"Oh, you mean you want to do this now?" Nana Abu asks.

"Yes, now."

"Okay, then. In that case why don't you choose whatever you like." Nana Abu puts his newspaper down.

I study all the things I brought and decide that painting rocks to decorate Naano's garden could be a good place to start. It'll look nice, especially since we did such an amazing job on the weeds.

"Let's paint these rocks," I say, holding up a few of the smooth rocks I brought with me.

Nana Abu chuckles.

I stare at him.

"Ahem." Nana Abu clears his throat. "You're serious."

"Of course, Nana Abu! This is a serious craft. As in arts and crafts," I explain.

"Right, right. Crafts. What do we do first?" Nana Abu pushes up the sleeves of his robe.

"Let's set up here," I say.

"Don't spill any paint on the table," Naano warns from the kitchen.

"Do you want to paint a rock too, Naano?" I offer.

"Maybe later," Naano says. Since she already has lots of hobbies, I don't push her.

Nana Abu rifles through the newspaper and pulls out some of the sections. Then he carefully spreads them out over the coffee table. He moves super slowly as he concentrates and folds the newspaper at the edges to make sure every inch of the wood is covered. Every now and then a headline catches his eye, and he pauses to read it.

"Ready?" I ask.

"Ready," Nana Abu finally agrees after what feels like forever.

"Do I get to do it too?" Zayd asks.

"Yes, Zayd," I sigh. "You're the whole reason I'm having this camp." That's mostly true. It's also to transform Nana Abu into a proper retired person.

"So, what do we do, exactly?" Nana Abu asks me.

"We paint the rocks with cool designs. I have these brushes and paints. And you can draw with marker or pencil first, if you want to make lines to fill in."

"I see. And then what do we do with these rocks when we're finished?" he asks.

"You can use them for lots of things. Like for a paperweight. Or a doorstop. But I thought we could decorate the garden with them."

"Very good." Nana Abu nods.

I lay out the paint and the brushes on the newspaper, pass out the rocks, and start to plan the design for my own rock in pencil first. It's a perfect gray oval with white specks, so I decide to paint it into a cute ladybug. I think I'll make it pink and black, or maybe bright blue with rainbow spots. . . .

"Done!" Nana Abu announces.

"What? You're done *already*?" I look up and see that he's painted his entire rock plain green. "Wait. Don't you want to do anything else to it?"

"Like what?"

"Like a design? Or some lettering? Maybe an inspirational message?"

"I like it this way. Just green." Nana Abu smiles. "But you can add something else to it if you want."

"I'm done too," Zayd says. His rock isn't even fully painted. There's just a big splotch of yellow on it.

"That's it, Zayd? What is that, even?"

"It's a yellow blob."

"I see that. Don't you want to add more to it?"

"No."

I miss my friends so much right now.

"Thank you for the nice craft," Nana Abu says as he picks up his paper and turns to the crossword puzzle.

The next thing I know, he's intently staring at the page. Painting rocks is clearly not going to be Nana Abu's hobby.

"What are we doing next?" Zayd turns to me.

I sigh and look at my notepad.

Chapter 8

* * *

"Okay, for our next craft we're going to reverse tie-dye these T-shirts," I say in my best cheerful counselor voice as I pull out a few old T-shirts that I packed into the suitcase.

"What is reverse tie-dying?" Nana Abu asks.

"Instead of adding colors to a white T-shirt, you take color *away* from a solid T-shirt with bleach," I explain.

"Why?" Nana Abu doesn't get it.

"To make a cool design. For fun. And because it looks good. And mostly because people do this at camp."

"But it's not safe for you to play with bleach. It's a very harsh chemical." Nana Abu shakes his head firmly. And I realize that he's probably right about that.

"How about if Zayd and I tie up the T-shirts with rubber bands, and you spray the bleach onto them for us?"

"I want to spray it," Zayd says. "I'm good at spraying."

Naano shuffles over to us when she overhears our conversation. She takes the T-shirt out of my hand and holds it up in the air.

"What are you going to do to this shirt? You're not cutting it," she says.

"No, we're not cutting it, Naano. We're bleaching it."

"Bleach? But it isn't stained. And it's red! You can't bleach a red shirt. Bleach is to make things white."

"I know. The bleach will make a pink design on it."

"Why are you going to ruin a perfectly good shirt? Your mother won't be happy with me."

"I asked her first. These are old shirts."

"Humph. They are old to you, but bilkul teek for someone else who needs them. Let's donate them." Ever since we convinced Naano to finally give away the things she'd been collecting in her basement, she's all about the donation center. She goes every month to give more things away. Mama is overjoyed about that.

"But—"

"And no wasting perfectly good bleach," she adds. "Find something else to do."

"Fine," I sigh. "I guess we can be done with craft time. What's next on the schedule? Let's see. Okay. Now we can start physical fitness."

"Like what?" Nana Abu seems worried.

"Do you want to practice juggling? Or go on a nature hike?"

Nana Abu smiles gently and pats my hand. "You and Zayd can do that. I'm going to rest for a bit."

"Okay, fine," I agree. Nana Abu did just do craft time. "Come on, Zayd," I call as Nana Abu shuffles back to the sofa and flips on the TV.

"I don't want to," Zayd says. "I want to watch TV too."

"But, Zayd," I argue. "I have all this stuff planned for us."

"I said I don't want to!" Zayd stands on the sofa and starts to sink between the cushions.

"You're not supposed to have so much screen time—"

"You're not the boss of me!" Zayd yells, starting to jump.

"It's okay," Nana Abu interrupts. "Let's see, what station—"

"Nickelodeon!" Zayd cheers. He takes the remote, finds the channel, and drops down next to Nana Abu on the couch.

"Zayd! I'm telling Mama. And I thought we were going to stick to the schedule," I complain.

But the two of them are completely zoned out watching cartoons and act like they don't even hear me.

"What about you, Naano? Want to do physical activity time with me?" I ask, even though I already know the answer. Naano mumbles something about making lunch and pats me on the back as she shuffles away. So I take a deep breath, go into Nana Abu's office, dial the phone, and wait until Jamal Mamoo answers.

My uncle is the greatest of all time, or as he likes to

call himself, the GOAT. He's sort of between a kid and an adult, even though he has an apartment and a job. He's super funny, and when he laughs, you can't help but join in. He's just the person I need to talk to right now.

"Salaam, Ami, how are you?" he says.

"It's not your mother. It's Zara."

"Oh. Hey, Zara. What's up?" Even through the phone, I can tell that my uncle is smiling.

I lower my voice so my grandparents can't hear me talking from the other room.

"You have to come help us," I say. "Please."

"Why?" Now I hear concern in Jamal Mamoo's voice. "What's going on?"

"Nothing. That's the problem," I explain.

"What do you mean? Is everything okay? Can you put Naano on the phone so I can talk to her?"

"I mean, Nana Abu is supposed to be retired, but he barely wants to do anything but read and watch TV. And Naano just wants to cook and clean and do chores and pray."

"Is that it?" Jamal Mamoo chuckles. "Tell me something I don't know."

"But, Mamoo, we were supposed to be here for Camp Naano and have a bunch of fun. And don't you think they should be into the stuff that old people do?"

"Like what?" Jamal Mamoo asks.

"I don't know. Like bird-watching and knitting and making scrapbooks."

"Don't *you* make scrapbooks? You're not *that* old," Jamal Mamoo says. I think he's teasing me, but I can't tell for sure.

"Mamoo, you've got to help me. I even planned out the whole week now, like a real camp counselor, but no one wants to do the things on my schedule. We barely did one craft. And now Zayd and Nana Abu are just sitting on the sofa watching TV. And I bet Naano is going to try to get me to help her with more cleaning. Can you come over?"

"I'm at work, Zara," Jamal Mamoo says. "But I can come by afterward if you'll still be there."

"I don't know, we might leave before then," I say.

"I'll come tomorrow, then," Jamal Mamoo offers. "I can get off early."

"Okay," I say, instantly more hopeful. Jamal Mamoo has a way of making everything better.

Chapter 9

* * *

I'm lying on the floor in the guest room, staring at my camp schedule and crossing out the things that no one wants to do, when Naano appears, standing over me.

"What are you doing?" she asks.

I scribble fiercely through "Make homemade ice cream" and don't respond.

"Why so down?" she insists.

"Because no one is listening to me!" I mumble.

"Hoi nehi sakhta," Naano says. "I'm listening to you right now."

"I mean, no one wants to do any of the things that I planned out, even though I worked really hard on the schedule," I clarify with a sniff. "Nana Abu isn't interested. And Zayd won't do what I say!" I get up and sit next to her on the bed.

"What do *you* want to do, beti?" Naano asks gently. She brushes the hair out of my face.

"The kinds of things Naomi is doing at her camp."

"Oh." Naano scratches her head. "Like what?"

"They get to go on field trips and have a talent show. And they're making homemade ice cream."

"Ice cream? That's so easy," Naano says. "You want to cook something? I'll teach you how to make a much harder dish."

"You mean for dinner, right?" I ask, suspicious that this is just another trick to get me to work.

"No, no, for fun," Naano says. "Come, let's go to the kitchen."

She starts to make her way out of the room, after smoothing out the bedspread again.

"So you're saying that we'll make treats, right?" I clarify.

"Sure."

"Do you think we should ask Zayd and Nana Abu to help us?" I'm still annoyed at Zayd, but it's probably the right thing to do.

Naano's eyebrows come together in concern. "Oh, no, no. Your grandfather makes too much mess when he's in the kitchen. And he doesn't follow the steps properly."

I nod sympathetically. That is the *worst*.

"But, Naano, look at them, just sitting there watching TV. You know, when you're retired, you're supposed to do all the things you don't have time for when you're working."

"He doesn't like cooking." Naano shakes her head, and I wonder if maybe she doesn't want to share the kitchen with Nana Abu.

"Okay, then what else do you think could be good hobbies for him? What *does* he like?"

"He likes having sweets and drinking chai. And being with his kids and grandkids. And telling stories from his childhood," Naano says.

I'm beginning to think Naano doesn't quite understand how hobbies work.

"But those aren't an activity, like making something, or playing a sport, or stuff like that," I explain.

"Humph," Naano grunts. She stares at me, and then glances over at Nana Abu, settled in the sofa, laughing at cartoons with Zayd. "He seems happy to me."

"I mean, yeah, I guess. Right now."

"But we can make an activity if you want. How about we have . . . a high tea," Naano suggests.

"A what?"

"High tea. Or you can just call it 'afternoon tea.'"

"You mean like when you and Nana Abu sit together and drink chai? Don't you already do that every afternoon?" I ask. I hold back a groan, because this seriously might be Naano's most unoriginal idea ever.

"Yes, but for this tea we'll make it fancy like a party, and have special sandwiches and patties, and cookies," Naano explains. "I used to host them for our friends when we were younger."

Like magic, Zayd suddenly appears when she says the word "cookies."

"I want cookies!" he says. "Where are they?"

"You'll have to help me make them, then," Naano says. "And set the table. And polish the good silver tea set."

Zayd turns to me with his mouth dropped open. This special tea totally sounds like a trick.

"What kind of cookies?" Zayd challenges. I can tell he's also deciding how to feel about this idea.

"The ones with jam inside." Naano casually mentions Zayd's favorites.

"Yum!" Zayd cheers.

At times like this I'm convinced my grandmother is some sort of genius.

"Should we start right now?" I ask.

"We'll have to plan it for tomorrow. I have to get some groceries," Naano says.

"Okay," I agree.

"And you have to wear something nice," Naano adds.

"Why?" Zayd asks.

"Because that's how afternoon tea works," Naano says. She glances over at Nana Abu. "Fancy clothes and no pajama parties."

And then she winks at me. Maybe Naano doesn't like seeing her husband in a bathrobe all day either. I guess afternoon tea can't be the worst thing ever. I'll add it to the schedule for tomorrow.

Chapter 10

* * *

"Are you hungry?" Mama asks as we pull up to the house. "I have to run back to the store to get tortillas."

"Is it Taco Tuesday? Yes!" Zayd whoops, jumping out of his seat. Today he's right, although he calls any day we have tacos "Taco Tuesday." It's hard to believe it's *still* Tuesday, since this week feels much longer than usual already.

"Can I go say hi to Naomi?" I ask.

"Sure, but then I could use your help with dinner." Mama covers up a yawn as she opens the garage to let us into the house.

I turn toward the Goldsteins', and Zayd starts to follow me.

"Go home, Zayd," I say.

"Are you going to the clubhouse?" Zayd asks. "I want to come too."

"Not now." I sigh. I've had enough of him for today. "Go see what Baba is doing."

"But—"

"I said no," I tell him firmly.

Zayd's face falls, and I feel a tiny pinch of guilt in my chest. But I really could use a break from him right now, and from thinking about how to keep him busy tomorrow.

"I'll see you in a little while, okay?" I add a little more gently.

"Fine." Zayd drags my roller suitcase across the concrete and takes it inside for me.

I ring the Goldsteins' doorbell, and Michael appears after a few moments.

"Hey," he says, stepping aside so I can come in.

"Is Naomi here?" I ask.

"In her room," he says.

67

I slip off my shoes, run upstairs, and find Naomi sprawled on her bed with a book.

"Hi," I say. "Why are you lying down?"

"I'm so sore," Naomi moans, rolling over to face me. "We were at the Adventure Park all day, and every part of my body hurts."

"Was it fun?" I ask, bracing myself to hear all about how amazing it was.

"Yeah, but—" Naomi pauses, and her face turns red.

"What?"

"I freaked out on the zip line. I didn't think I was afraid of heights, but all of a sudden I couldn't do it. I was standing there, looking down, and I felt like I couldn't breathe."

"Oh, sorry," I say. That sounds terrible.

"It's okay. My partners were nice about it. And now I'm going to practice climbing trees until I get over my fear," Naomi says. She sits up, hugs her knees to her chest, and nods thoughtfully. "And then we can go back together, you and me."

"Deal." It's seriously impressive how Naomi never backs down from a challenge.

"What about you?" Naomi asks. "How was Camp Zara?"

"Not so great," I admit. "Zayd was being hyper. And my grandfather doesn't seem interested in finding a new hobby. Naano wouldn't let us tie-dye."

"What about the physical activity part?" Naomi asks. "Did you make an obstacle course?"

"Not yet."

"Scavenger hunt?"

"Maybe tomorrow. After the special tea my grandmother is making us have," I share, remembering.

"What do you mean 'special'? Like lavender?" Naomi wrinkles her nose. "Flowery tea is gross."

"No, Naano says we have to get dressed up and use fancy dishes and drink chai and eat tea foods."

"That could be fun," Naomi says encouragingly.

"Yeah, but it's not really an activity."

"Sure it is. As long as you're all doing it together and having a good time. Isn't that one of your rules?"

"I guess."

"Then it sounds like an activity to me. Is Zayd doing it too?"

"He has no choice."

Naomi smiles. "Well, make sure you take pictures. And bring me some of those cookies if your grandma makes them. The jam ones."

"I'm sure she'd love to send you some," I promise.

Seeing Naomi get excited about tea makes it suddenly better. Maybe we just need to go all in on this idea. Together.

"Hey, you two!" Michael yells from the bottom of the stairs. "Gloria is here with Popsicles."

"Paletas," I hear Gloria correct him. "Pineapple, mango, and pineapple mango."

We race down the stairs, Naomi suddenly finding a burst of energy.

Gloria is standing on the lawn with a container full of bright orange and yellow fruit bars. Jade dipped the ends of the Popsicle sticks into paint, of course, and added a Thomas family logo that she came up with.

"They're beautiful!" I say, admiring my creative friends' handiwork. "Thank you!"

I hurry home for tacos, and to get the paletas into the freezer before they melt. One for me and another for Zayd. They'll be the perfect end to the meal, and to the day.

Chapter 11

* * *

The next morning, before we leave for Naano's, Mama searches through her closet and pulls out a mint-green dress with a million ruffles.

"How's this?" she asks me. It's about my size.

"Where did you get that?" I ask.

"I was saving it for a special occasion," Mama says. "What do you think?"

"Ummm." I examine the clean white leggings and blue T-shirt with strawberries on it that I'm wearing. "But I'm already dressed." My outfit seems perfect for Naano's tea party.

"You don't like the dress?" Mama's face droops.

"It's okay," I quickly say. "It just doesn't look very comfy."

"Oh, you'll be fine." Mama is instantly cheerful again. "You can change out of it after the tea."

"Are you coming?"

"I wish I could, love, but I have to be at that training."

"Do we really have to dress up *that* much?" I protest.

"Naano wants it to be special. She called me this morning to make sure you and Zayd remembered to wear nice clothes."

"Fine." I take the dress and stuff it into my suitcase.

"Add these, too," Mama says, handing me a clip-on bow tie and a button-down shirt for Zayd.

When we arrive, Nana Abu opens the door for us, and he's wearing a nice shirt and pants. Naano's in the kitchen shredding a pile of chicken.

"Salaam, Naano," Zayd says. "We brought dress-up clothes."

"Good boy," Naano says. "You two, have some cereal." I guess she didn't have time to make us breakfast.

"You're going to be extra good, Zayd, right?" I whisper

to him as I get out some bowls for us. "This is important to Naano."

"I know," Zayd says, nodding his head. "I'm ready."

While we're eating, Naano walks to her china cabinet and takes out a carved silver tea set that's blackish, a bottle of polish, and some cotton balls.

"This is for you to clean, Zayd, if you're done eating," she says, setting him up to polish the set at the counter.

"I know, I know," Zayd moans as he climbs onto a stool. But after a while he yells, "This is cool!" He holds up a blackened cotton ball. "Check out all this black stuff coming off!"

Next, Naano and I make the butter cookie dough. I roll the dough into balls and flatten them onto a cookie sheet. When Zayd's done polishing, he gets to drop a spoonful of strawberry jam into the middle of each.

Nana Abu shuffles into the kitchen while Naano and I are making the filling for tea sandwiches. It's the shredded chicken mixed with tiny pieces of celery and mayonnaise.

"Want to help us, Nana Abu?" I ask, ignoring Naano's

glare. If she's letting Zayd help in here, there's no reason not to let her husband join in too.

"Sure," Nana Abu agrees. He settles into the chair next to me. "What should I do?"

"Cut the crust off this bread," Naano grunts. "Carefully."

She hands him a loaf, and we make an assembly line. Nana Abu passes me the slices of bread with the crusts cut off. I spread some of the chicken salad onto the slice, and then Naano tops it with another slice and cuts it diagonally. She layers rows of the sandwiches on a plate and covers them with a damp dish towel to keep them from drying.

"Good job cutting, Nana Abu," I say, cheering him on like I imagine a camp counselor would.

"Thanks." Nana Abu smiles.

"Don't you think you'd like to do more cooking, Nana Abu?" I ask, which makes Naano glare at me again.

"Well, this isn't exactly cooking," Nana Abu says. "It's more like assembling. But that suits me better anyway. I prefer to build things."

"Really? Like what?" I ask.

"Oh, I used to make many things like picture frames and lamps. Back when I had steadier hands."

"You did?" I've never heard this before.

"Oh, yes," Naano chimes in. "Your Nana Abu is very good at building. He put up the fence in the backyard too." She pats Nana Abu's arm proudly. "All by himself."

"Wow." I'm impressed, and surprised. I wonder what other things Nana Abu can do that I know nothing about. Why doesn't anybody ever tell me anything?

But before I can ask for more details, the doorbell rings.

Chapter 12

✳ ✳ ✳

"It's Jamal Mamoo!" Zayd yells after he runs to the door and peeks through the window on the side.

"You came!" I jump up to greet my uncle as he walks into the house. Zayd is clinging to him like he's afraid Jamal Mamoo will disappear.

"Salaam, salaam!" Jamal Mamoo says. He bends down to kiss his mom and dad before giving me a hug. "I told you I'd get off early today."

"Now you can have high tea with us," Naano says.

"'Hi' tea? How about 'hey' tea? Or maybe 'what's up' tea?" Jamal Mamoo says.

"She's serious," I whisper.

"Oh. In that case I'd be delighted," Jamal Mamoo says. He turns to me and shrugs.

Nana Abu leaves to shave and get ready while the rest of us follow Naano's orders to set up the dining table. I spread out a stiff flowery tablecloth. Jamal Mamoo arranges fancy gold-rimmed teacups and saucers at all the places, instead of the regular worn mugs they normally use for chai. Then we add little plates, cloth napkins, and the special forks and spoons Naano usually saves for parties.

We stand back and admire the table setting. It is special.

"All of this just for little old me?" Jamal Mamoo jokes. "This is very elegant. But where's the food? I'm starving."

"We eat *after* we get ready," Naano commands. She stares at Jamal Mamoo, who's still dressed in blue scrubs from the place where he works taking X-rays and other pictures of people's insides. "Did you bring other clothes?"

Jamal Mamoo busts out his extra-loud wacky laugh. "No, Ami. I didn't get the invitation until two seconds ago. But I'll see what I can find."

I change into my ruffly dress and try to ignore how itchy it is around my neck. Then I help Zayd clip on his bow tie and brush his hair.

Naano shuffles into her room to get dressed. When she comes out, she's in a pink shalwar kameez, her hair is all fluffed up, and she's wearing lipstick.

"You look really nice, Naano," I say, suddenly glad I had something packed to wear, especially since I spilled cereal on my leggings during breakfast.

"Thank you. Let me plait your hair," she says.

I try to stand still while Naano yanks on my hair and twists it into two braids.

"Perfect for afternoon tea with the boss," she says, stepping back to admire her work.

"Who's the boss?" I ask.

"Me, of course." Naano winks. "Who else?"

When we go back to the dining room, Jamal Mamoo

has found a shirt and tie and is wearing them over his scrubs. The shirt is too short in the arms, and the tie is extra wide, but he grins at me.

"Very nice," he says as he pulls a chair out for me. "Shall we take some tea, madam?"

"Yes, we shall!" I say with a curtsy.

"Whoa!" Zayd says as Nana Abu comes into the room. His scruffy white beard is gone, and he smells like his after-shave cologne. He's wearing a black suit with a red tie, and a folded handkerchief is sticking out of his pocket. When he gets closer, I notice that he even has a tie clip with a little jewel on it, and silver buttons on his shirt sleeves.

"Looking sharp, Abu," Jamal Mamoo says.

"Your mother made me," Nana Abu says, which makes everyone laugh.

"That's right," Naano adds. "Your Nana Abu was always the most handsome man at our tea parties. He told the best stories. And everyone loved my sandwiches and tea cookies. Our friends always said I should open a restaurant."

Her eyes gleam with the memories, and I imagine

Naano behind the counter of a restaurant, yelling out orders. It would have been a perfect job for her.

Zayd and I follow Naano into the kitchen and help carry the food to the table. Then Naano brings out the steaming hot pot of tea. She pours it for the grown-ups. Then she goes back into the kitchen and returns with a smaller teapot and pours something into Zayd's and my cups.

"Hot chocolate?" Zayd asks, lighting up when he sees it.

"Yes, just for you, skinny mouse."

Even better, there's a little bowl of halal marshmallows.

"So, what prompted all this?" Jamal Mamoo asks as we pass around the plates of food. I nibble my sandwich and wipe the corners of my mouth with my napkin like I see people do on TV when they're being formal.

"Zara wanted to do an activity," Naano explains.

Jamal Mamoo turns to me. "This was your idea?" he asks. "Nice one."

"Well, not completely," I confess. "This wasn't on my

schedule until Naano said we should do it. I was telling Naano that we should do more active things. You know, like I was talking to you about yesterday." I tilt my head in the direction of Nana Abu when he isn't watching.

"Ah. Right." Jamal Mamoo nods. "Interesting choice." He pops an entire sandwich into his mouth and chews it.

"You're supposed to take delicate bites, like Zara," Naano scolds. "And, Zayd, hold your teacup like this." Naano sticks out her pinky finger as she grips the handle of her cup.

"Why?" Zayd asks, and fishes a marshmallow out of his cup with his tongue.

"Because this is high tea," Naano explains. "You can't eat like a budhoo when you have high tea."

"Why don't you have teas with your friends anymore?" Jamal Mamoo asks.

"Oh, I don't know. Everyone is tired. Or moved away. Or is busy watching their grandchildren." Naano's eyes scan Zayd and me when she says the last part.

Nana Abu watches all of us with an amused expression

and quietly eats a couple of sandwiches, a cookie, and lots of halwa. He drinks his chai and then folds his napkin and pushes back his chair.

"Thank you, all. That was very tasty," he says politely.

It's like the green painted rock all over again! He's not supposed to be done with this activity so quickly. When I see Naano's face fall, I recognize her disappointment and decide to do something to keep the tea going.

"Wait a minute, Nana Abu. How about you tell us a story?" I ask.

"And, here, have some more chai," Jamal Mamoo offers.

Nana Abu slides his cup across the table toward him and then turns to ask me, "What kind of story?"

"I don't know. Can you tell us about how you built that fence all by yourself?" I ask. I am honestly curious about how he managed do to that, especially when I remember him trying to pull weeds. Did he wear a toolbelt? Did he use actual tools?

"Okay, I can tell you." Nana Abu leans back and starts to talk about how he measured the yard, bought all the

supplies from the hardware store, and dug the holes for the
fence posts. As he speaks, I watch his eyes light up.

"I hit my thumb with the hammer once. It swelled up
to twice its normal size. But other than that, it all went
pretty smoothly," he says with a chuckle.

As I listen to him lovingly describe the different types
of nails he used, one thing becomes perfectly clear. I need
to get him building things again.

Chapter 13

"Can he build us a tree house?" Zayd jumps up and down at the thought. "I've always wanted a tree house. With a rope ladder!"

"No, Zayd," Jamal Mamoo laughs. "Nana Abu is not getting up on ladders or in trees at his age. Think smaller."

We're huddled together with our uncle in the family room, coming up with plans, now that I've told them my idea.

"How about a clubhouse on the ground?" I suggest.

Even though we already have one at Naomi's house, it might be fun to have one here, too.

"Smaller," Jamal Mamoo repeats.

"Um . . . a birdhouse?" I ask.

"Perfect." Jamal Mamoo nods his head. "Good thinking."

"Nana Abu can build it for us, and then we can paint it and decorate it!" I add.

"We can use the glitter glue!" Zayd says. He runs over to the suitcase and holds up a tube of pink glitter. "And these sparkly tassels."

"Look at you two," Jamal Mamoo says, and turns to me. "I'm impressed by your preparation. I've personally never seen a blinged-out birdhouse before, but why not? Just make sure it won't make the birds sick if they eat the decorations."

"Good point."

"We can make it the best and biggest birdhouse ever!" Zayd says. He runs over to Nana Abu, who's sitting in his armchair dozing after high tea. "Wake up, Nana Abu!

We're going to make a birdhouse! A big one. It'll be a bird mansion!"

"You want to make something? That's nice. I can help you," Nana Abu mumbles sleepily.

"No, Abu, we need *you* to make it for us. None of us know how to work with wood," Jamal Mamoo says.

"But I don't have any materials," Nana Abu says, more alert now. "Or a design."

"That's what the internet is for!" Jamal Mamoo says. "Zara is going to find instructions on how to make a nice birdhouse."

"A bird mansion!" Zayd corrects.

Naano walks into the room then. She's got her apron on over her fancy shalwar kameez and seems tired after all the hard work of making the tea and cleaning up, even though we helped her with everything. Zayd and I put away the leftovers and dried all the teacups. And I packed up a container of jam cookies to deliver to Naomi.

"What are you all doing?" Naano asks.

"We're going to build a birdhouse with Nana Abu," I say. "You like feeding the birds, right?"

"Yes, but are you going to make a big mess? I just finished cleaning, and I don't want a mess." Naano doesn't look confident in our abilities.

"We'll work in the garage, don't worry," Jamal Mamoo promises.

Next my uncle helps me find a website that has step-by-step instructions on how to build a birdhouse with a slanted roof, a hole, and a little perch.

"It says here that this type of house is good for blue-birds and swallows," he reads. "They live in this area. So that sounds good to me."

I print out the list of items we need, which we all agree is the first rule of any craft project. And then Nana Abu approves the design.

"I should be able to do that," he says.

"It's going to be the most amazing birdhouse ever!" Zayd cheers.

"All right. Let's go to the craft store," Jamal Mamoo says. He points at my frilly dress and then adds, "You might want to change first."

"Can we go to Carmen's after?" Zayd adds.

"Why not?"

Zayd runs over to me and gives me a squeeze. I'm glad he's excited about a craft.

"Raspberry gelati!" he whoops. "Are you coming, Naano?"

"I'm too tired. I'm going to watch my dramas," Naano says. "But bring me mango ice, please."

"You got it," Jamal Mamoo says.

We pile into Jamal Mamoo's car to set out on our craft store adventure, and then to get the best frozen custard and shaved ice in town. Not bad for a day at Camp Zara, even if it's not what I had planned. I can be flexible.

Nana Abu clicks on his seat belt and turns to look at me in the back seat. He's lost the jacket and tie but is still wearing his nice shirt and pants. And he already feels more like the grandfather I've always known.

"Ready?" he asks with a smile.

"Ready!" I smile back.

Chapter 14

* * *

Zayd picks up the birdhouse and turns it over in his hand.

"It's so tiny," he says. "How will a bird family have any room in here?"

"Shush, Zayd," I say. "It's really nice, Nana Abu."

It's taken Nana Abu half the morning to make this. It's like he's moving in slow motion, even though he's not. He acted the same way at the craft store yesterday. He picked up every piece of wood and turned it over five times before finally putting something into the cart. Then he thought about it for a while before moving to the next item on the list. It took so long that Zayd and I made up a scavenger hunt in the fake flower section. We totally earned the trip to Carmen's by the time we finally left. And it was worth getting scolded by Mama for ruining our appetites when Jamal Mamoo dropped us home at dinnertime with watermelon- and raspberry-ice-stained mouths. Although I have to admit, Gloria's paletas are almost as good.

I take the birdhouse and turn it over. It is a little on the small side, but otherwise perfect. All the edges line up, and the nails are hammered in neat and straight lines.

"Should we make a bigger one next?" Nana Abu asks us. His hands are covered with sawdust, but he turns to me and smiles.

"Can we?" I ask. "Do you have enough wood?"

"I bought plenty, in case I made a mistake," Nana Abu says.

"Let's make a huge one!" Zayd says. "A bird mansion for real!"

"We can try," Nana Abu agrees. "Now that I know what I'm doing, it will go faster."

For the bird mansion, we decide to connect a few of the smaller birdhouses. That way it'll be like one gigantic house with different rooms.

"Maybe it's more like a bird hotel," Nana Abu says.

"Where will we hang it up? Won't it be too heavy to hang on a tree branch?" I ask.

"I thought we would have it sit on a pole in the yard," Nana Abu says.

Nana Abu makes three more birdhouses while Zayd and I take turns helping him hold pieces, supply him with lemonade, and read the newspaper to him. Each one he makes takes less time than the last. Nana Abu hums while he works and sticks his tongue out a little when he measures.

"And now we just have to attach them to each other," he finally says.

"How?" I ask.

"Let's use wood glue and nails to be sure it's secure."

Nana Abu speaks like an expert. "And then you can paint and decorate it however you want."

Zayd and I were talking about glitter and tassels yesterday, but now that I see the finished house, I want to go for a simpler look.

"If it's sitting in the front of the house, maybe we should match it and use the same colors," I suggest.

"White with black shutters and a red door?" Zayd asks. "That's so boring. How about purple and green with a yellow door?"

"I think it'll be cuter to match the house, don't you?" I ask.

"I guess," Zayd says, sounding unconvinced.

"We can make the pole striped if you want?"

"Okay," Zayd agrees.

We put on the first coat of paint before lunch and let it dry while we eat.

"You've been busy out in the garage today," Naano says. I can't tell if she's happy that we are out of her way or if she's missing us.

"You can help us, Naano," I offer.

"I'll help when you're done," Naano says.

"When we're done?" I ask. "What are you going to do then?"

"Invite the birds," Naano says. "And feed them."

"You can make it a nest-and-breakfast," Nana Abu says, and smiles.

"Right!" Zayd laughs so hard, he snorts. "We should make tiny pancakes!"

After lunch we paint fake shutters onto the birdhouses with black paint. We make the perches red, since there's a hole instead of doors. Zayd is still so excited to use glitter that we sprinkle some onto the roof after we paint it brown. It's extra nice, with a bit of shimmer that catches the sunlight.

Finally the bird mansion-hotel is complete, and Nana Abu digs the pole into the ground.

"Just like when he built the fence," Naano says proudly as she watches. When he's done attaching the birdhouse, I suggest we take pictures to send to Jamal Mamoo and Mama.

"Nana Abu," I call out to him. "Go stand next to it."

My grandfather straightens up extra tall next to his project, folding his arms like a pro. Then Zayd jumps in, and Naano wants to join too. We end up taking a selfie with all of us.

Our craft time ended up taking the entire day. But it was the best day of spring break so far. That's because Nana Abu is full of life again.

Chapter 15

* * *

"Are you open for business? I have some books I'd love to add," the woman walking her tiny dog past the house says as we finish up our little photo shoot.

"Pardon me?" Nana Abu asks.

"I'm sorry." The lady stops. "Isn't that a Little Free Library?"

"No, it's a birdhouse," Zayd says. He motions toward the dog. "Can I pet your dog, please?"

"Yes, of course. Captain is friendly. What a ... um ... *large* birdhouse. Did you build it yourself?" The woman smiles at us and pushes up her glasses as Zayd rubs her little black-and-white furball behind the ears.

"It's actually a bird hotel," Zayd explains. "For lots of bird families. My grandpa made it."

"How creative," the woman says. She then turns to Nana Abu. "You're very talented. We could use your skills over at the Senior Center."

"The what?" I ask while my grandfather blushes uncomfortably from the praise.

"The Senior Center," the woman repeats, a little louder. "Are you not familiar with it?"

"No, we never heard of it," Naano says.

"Oh, well, you would love it, I'm sure. The center offers all sorts of classes for seniors—everything from ballroom dancing and Zumba to computers. There are social events and field trips and movie nights," the woman gushes.

"Okay, thank you very much," Naano says politely, in a way that I can tell means she isn't interested. It's the same tone she uses when she answers the phone and talks to people who try to sell her things.

"You're welcome. I volunteer at the center, so I'm there a lot, and I'm always talking it up," the woman says. "Hope to see you soon. Nice to meet you."

"You too. Bye-bye." Nana Abu waves.

"Can anyone go to the center?" I pipe up before the woman walks away.

"Well, it's intended for seniors, and the classes and activities are for an over-fifty-five crowd, but anyone is welcome," she says. "I'm sure everyone would be delighted to have some young visitors."

"How much does it cost?" I ask.

"Visiting the center is free, and most of the programs are free. There's a small fee and registration for classes and for the gym."

Gym? How big *is* this place?

"I hope you'll come by." The woman smiles again and begins to walk away as Captain starts to run ahead and tug on his leash. "We were recently talking about putting up a Little Free Library and would welcome your help. This bird . . . hotel is fantastic."

"Thank you," Nana Abu says. He bows his head slightly and touches his hand to his heart.

As I watch the lady and Captain head down the street, I can't believe what I just heard! The Senior Center sounds like an even better version of Har Shalom camp—for my grandparents. And it's *free*? Baba always says that nothing in life is free, and I can't wait to tell him about this.

"You should totally go!" I turn to Naano. "The Senior Center sounds amazing!"

"Dekhengey," Naano mumbles, which is her favorite way of saying "We'll see."

"But don't you think it sounds perfect? Especially since you're retired? You can do so many different activities, and make new friends," I continue.

"Yes, it sounds nice. Let's go inside now and have some chai," Nana Abu says.

"Let me find you a pack of those ginger biscuits," Naano adds. The two of them turn around and rush inside. I can't remember the last time I saw them move so fast.

"Come, Zayd," Naano calls behind her. "You need to wash your hands."

Zayd looks at me and shrugs. "They aren't going to go," he says.

"We can convince them," I say. "It sounds perfect for them. Nana Abu can help over there and find more hobbies. He'll be like Mr. Chapman in no time. And I'm sure there's something that Naano would like to try too."

"Maybe," Zayd says. "But I know they won't."

I have a feeling Zayd is right. But not if I can find a way to convince them. If I have anything to do with it, Camp Zara is moving over to the Senior Center.

Chapter 16

* * *

"Ready to go?" Baba asks when I come downstairs. "I'm dropping you off at Naano's today. Mama had to go into work extra early."

"Almost," I say. I pull on my sneakers with the sparkly laces. They match the sparkle on my Niagara Falls T-shirt. And I even put on a puffy skirt.

"Interesting get-up," Baba says, eyeing my outfit. "Very shiny. Let me guess. Another high tea today?"

"No, we're going to the Senior Center. Don't older people love waterfalls?" I thought it might be a good way to start conversations.

"Why yes, they probably do. But did you say *you're* going to the Senior Center?"

"Hopefully," I say. "If Nana Abu and Naano agree."

"I need to hear more about this in the car," Baba says. "Come on, Zayd. Let's go!"

On the way to Naano's, I update Baba on what Captain's owner told us about the place, and how badly I want to take my grandparents there.

"Are you sure you don't want to go there for yourself?" Baba asks as he eyes me in his rearview mirror. "Because I hope you realize that it's actually designed for older people, not kids your age."

I consider what my father is saying. Yes, the Senior Center sounds like a super-fantastic place where there are literally camp activities going on all the time. And, yes, I'm curious to see it for myself. But I understand that it's not for me and Zayd. I'm like a camp counselor now, and this can be our first field trip!

"I'm sure," I say. "It's for them. I think they need to check it out. If they like it, maybe it can be somewhere that they start to go together. Especially when Zayd and I are back in school."

"Well, good for you for supporting your grandparents. But are they keen to go? Because to be honest, it doesn't sound like them," Baba says.

"They will be," I say. I look over at Zayd, and we do our secret handshake. We've got our plan to convince them all worked out.

"Okay, then, have fun, and be good. This is your last day of spring break. Can you believe it? The week flew by so fast. Love you both," Baba says as we jump out of the car.

"Love you too," we say, and I race Zayd to the door.

Nana Abu opens the door dressed in a shalwar kameez and vest.

"Asalaamualaikum. Jumuah Mubarak!" he says.

"Waalaikumasalaam," Zayd says. "I like your outfit. Are you wearing that to the Senior Center?"

"No, to the masjid," Nana Abu replies, and smiles. "It's Friday, so we'll go for jumuah prayers."

"And then to the Senior Center?" Zayd asks.

"I thought we would take you to lunch afterward," Nana Abu says. "Where would you like to go?"

"Pizza!" Zayd says. "Oooh, can we go to Chuck E. Cheese!"

Zayd has obviously forgotten our plan already.

"You mean pizza, and then the Senior Center?" I add, giving him the eye.

"Right, I mean to the Senior Center," Zayd says quickly. He turns to me and whispers, "I got this."

"Oh ho, what's all this about the Senior Center? Choro, nah." Naano comes shuffling toward us. "Come in, let's have breakfast."

We sit at the table and eat another one of Naano's special breakfasts. This time it's a fluffy omelet filled with gooey cheese. Even Zayd gobbles it up. When we're done, we get right back to working on our grandparents again.

"So, can we go? Can we PLEASE go to the Senior Center?" Zayd starts.

"Yeah, can you take us? It sounds like so much fun, and we really want to see it," I add.

Nana Abu takes a sip of his chai and turns to Naano. "What is wrong with these children today?" he asks, concern in his voice.

"Moojay nehi patta," Naano says. She throws up her hands.

"Nothing is wrong with us!" I giggle. "It's just that it's our last day here, and we want to do something special with you."

"Jumuah is special," Naano argues. "The high tea was special. The birdhouse was special. Nashukray bachay."

"That's all great, but we wanted to do something else. Something new, and different, for all of us. And the Senior Center sounds so awesome." I pause, and glance at Zayd. "And when we get back, you'll be tired, so you can rest while Zayd and I organize the pantry," I add.

"I'll do all the cans!" Zayd promises, following my lead. "PLEEEEEAAAASE?"

Nana Abu looks at Naano and lifts an eyebrow. "I guess we could stop by on the way home," he says.

"For five minutes," Naano grumbles. "I have so many

things to do. And the pantry will take them a while."

"Yes!" Zayd turns around, and we slap hands and do our handshake again.

We did it! I have a good feeling that it's going to be as awesome as we think it will be.

"First help me clean up a little before we go," Naano says. "Zayd, you sweep the floor. And, Zara, please wipe the table."

This time we don't even mind.

Chapter 17

* ✳ *

The man in the black kufi hands Zayd
a slice of pizza on a paper plate.

"For you, little man," he says.

He then holds a plate out for me. "Would you like a
slice?" he asks.

"Thank you," I say, taking it with a smile.

I guess we're having lunch at the mosque, because after
prayers Zayd ran straight to the man with the pizza. And
there are so many other people sharing food. A lady is
scooping out bowls of chicken and rice with a yogurt sauce.

Another has colorful mithai to celebrate her son's engagement. And a teenager is passing out bags of chips from a gigantic box. It kind of feels like a carnival.

Naano and I prayed together. She was sitting on a chair in the prayer hall, while I sat on the soft green carpet. We listened to the imam talk about being kind to others and not waiting for people to ask us for help. When we were done with prayer, Naano met a few of her friends and was talking to them for a long time. Then we finally put our shoes back on and came outside.

Now she and Nana Abu are sitting on a bench, sharing a bowl of rice. Everyone who walks by greets them and has a conversation. When we're done eating, Zayd and I play on the swing set for a while until they're ready to go.

"Do you kids want to get anything else to eat?" Nana Abu asks as we get into my grandparents' car.

"I'm full," Zayd says.

"Me too," I add.

"Okay, so what now?" Naano asks. "Should we go home and rest?"

"No," Zayd says. "We're going to the Senior Center, remember?"

"You still want to do that?" Naano asks, adjusting the dupatta on her head. "You're not tired?"

"Nope," I say. "We're not tired. And remember, you promised we would go!"

"Did we? Chalo," Naano says to Nana Abu. "A promise is a promise."

The drive to the Senior Center is quick. When we pull up into the driveway, we see a boxy brown brick building. After the big bronze dome and arched windows of the mosque, it's a lot smaller than I imagined. And to be honest, it looks a lot like our elementary school.

"Here we are," Nana Abu says. "What should we do?"

Now that we're here, I suddenly realize that I have no idea at all what we're supposed to do. At the mosque we all knew exactly where to go and how to act. Plus there were plenty of people we knew to talk to and play with. Here none of us knows anything about this place, anyone here, or what to expect.

No wonder my grandparents were nervous or uncomfortable about coming. And now I am too. Just a little.

"Let's go inside and look around," I suggest after taking a deep breath. "If you don't like it, we can leave." Mama always said that to me whenever I was about to start a new class or activity. I liked having that option, although I never chose to leave. I did come close once with my tap dance lessons.

We walk inside, past two sets of sliding glass doors, into a brightly lit room with a reception desk. There's a woman sitting behind it, and a gray-haired man walks down the hallway and greets us on his way out the door.

"First time here?" the man asks us. I guess it's obvious. I nod my head. "Marissa will be happy to show you around. Welcome."

"Well, hello there." Marissa waves us over to her desk when she sees us. "How can I help you today?"

"We wanted to check out the center," I volunteer. "For them. My grandparents."

"I see. That's lovely. And that's what we're here for."

Marissa smiles brightly. "Do your grandparents speak English?"

"Yes," Naano says, coming closer to the desk. "We speak English. And Urdu. And Punjabi."

"Wonderful!" Marissa says. "Well, it's nice to meet you. Are you here for classes, events, social hours, the gym?"

"We don't know," Naano says. "We just wanted to see what things you have."

Marissa seems thrilled that someone finally asked. She whips out some papers with monthly calendars on them that have different activities printed on each day. It's basically like my camp schedule, but more official-looking.

"You see here is today's date. We had computer class this morning, table tennis club, bridge club, and a balance wellness workshop. This afternoon there's walking club, which takes place right here inside the building if it rains, and tonight there's bingo."

"I see," Naano says. I can tell she's feeling a little overwhelmed by all the information, even though she likes making lists and plans like me. "Thank you very much."

"Chalo?" she says to Nana Abu, which I know means "Should we go?" Marissa seems to realize it too.

"Why don't I walk you around our facility," she suggests. "And you can get a sense of the space, and more of what we offer."

"That's okay," Nana Abu says. "We don't want to trouble you. Have a nice day."

And just like that, they're choosing to leave! Now I wish I'd never said they could leave if they didn't like it here. That's just supposed to make you feel better, not something you actually decide to do! I have to think of a way to get them to stay for a bit longer—and quick.

Chapter 18

* * *

"I need the bathroom," I say, tugging on Naano's sleeve. It's a not a lie—I *did* drink a big bottle of water with my pizza and could use a bathroom break.

"Can't you wait until we get home?" Naano whispers.

"Noooo," I whine. That part might be a teeny tiny lie. I might be able to wait. But I start to fidget and act desperate anyway.

"The restrooms are down the hall to the left, sweetie," Marissa says. "Come, we can walk with you, and I'll show you all around on the way."

Yes! It worked!

We head down the hallway and pass a large ballroom on the right with a small stage and an American flag in the corner.

"This is where bingo happens every Friday night, so they'll be setting up for that soon," Marissa says. "But this is also where dance and exercise classes are held, like yoga and aerobics."

"Very nice," Nana Abu says politely. I know he has no interest in any of those things. *Come on, Marissa.* I try to send her a telepathic message. *Show them something they'll like!*

"Here's the gym to our left. We have personal trainers available," she says next.

Through the window I see a few people on treadmills and using weight machines. That is definitely not going to be it.

"Cool!" Zayd says as he smooshes his face against the glass and waves to a woman doing biceps curls. "You can watch everyone work out."

"Here we have our lounge, and back there you'll find table tennis and a pool table," Marissa says as she motions toward the back of the hall.

"Those ladies look nice, Naano," I say, pointing to a group of women who are passing around a thermos and plastic containers in a corner of the lounge.

"Oh yes, Mrs. Sharma, Mrs. Rosenblatt, and Mrs. Lee are regulars here. They like to have tea together, and they always bring the best treats to share with the staff. I just love Mrs. Sharma's Indian pastries. They're the best I've ever had!"

"I make pastries too," Naano shares. I smile, because there's no way Naano is going to let this Mrs. Sharma outdo her in the cooking department.

"Really? I bet they're delicious too. Let me introduce you," Marissa says. She points. "There's the restroom right over by the water fountain, sweetie."

I go into the bathroom and take an extra-long time. After I sing three songs while washing my hands, I redo my ponytail. Then I make faces at myself in front of the giant mirror and practice a dance move Gloria taught me. And after it feels like enough time has gone by, I finally leave.

When I come out, Naano is sitting on a chair with the ladies, and they are chatting like old friends. I watch as one of them passes a container to Naano, who breaks off a piece of a cookie and tastes it. Her eyes widen, and I can tell she isn't faking when she says how good it is.

"This reminds me of a biscuit my mother made when I was a child," she says. "Speaking of child," she says, motioning for me to come forward, "this is my granddaughter."

"Look at you. Aren't you adorable!" one of the ladies says.

"Nice T-shirt. I just love Niagara Falls. Have you been?" another asks.

"You keeping your grandparents company today?" the third adds.

I act as charming as possible and answer all their questions. Then I turn to Naano and speak extra loudly, so they can all hear. "Naano, you should come again, and bring some of your nankhatai for them to try."

"Nankhatai!" The lady who I'm guessing is Mrs. Sharma gasps. "I haven't tasted those in years! Please do come back on Monday and have tea with us."

"We play cards too," her friend adds. "If you enjoy that."

"Naano is really good at cards," I volunteer. I leave out the part about her trying to cheat. "And she always wins at Monopoly."

The ladies gush:

"You must come Monday."

"We would love to play with you."

"There's so much to do here."

Naano seems overwhelmed by the attention, but in a good way. She tells the ladies that she would love to come again, and I'm confident that she isn't pretending.

"Where are Zayd and Nana Abu?" I ask.

"Marissa took them out those doors to the back," she says. "Go find them."

She doesn't come with me, which is another good sign that she's enjoying herself.

I catch up with Zayd and Nana Abu outside, and Marissa is pointing at a bunch of plants growing in wooden boxes.

"This is our community garden project. Everyone chips in to plant, water, and weed it. Do you like to garden?" she asks.

"Oh no, we hate weeding," Zayd says quickly.

Marissa laughs. "It's hard work, but some people enjoy it. Maybe you'd prefer to harvest instead?"

"Someone told us you wanted to build a Little Free Library?" I ask.

"Why yes!" Marissa turns and smiles at me. "We just discussed it during our last volunteer meeting. We need someone to lead the effort."

I point at Nana Abu, but he is suddenly finding some plant in the garden fascinating and is touching one of the leaves.

"He's good at building. He built us a giant birdhouse—"

"A bird hotel," Zayd interrupts.

"A big birdhouse that looks like a Little Free Library," I continue after glaring at Zayd. "He can help."

"That would be amazing," Marissa gushes. "Sir, would you like to join our volunteer committee?"

Nana Abu looks at Marissa, who is nodding her head so much that I'm afraid she might hurt herself. Then he looks at me, sighs, and gives me a little smile. "If you like," he says. "This little one has been pushing me to be more active and have a new hobby. So, I guess I can try to do something that will help others."

"Wonderful!" Marissa claps her hands. "Nice work," she adds, giving me an appreciative nod that I'm pretty sure is reserved for camp-counselor-type people like us.

"Thanks," I say, feeling good about myself.

Zayd grabs my hand, and we do a little victory dance behind the two of them as we walk back inside.

"Can we go now?" Zayd asks when we get back to Naano, who's telling a story and making her new friends laugh.

"We'll go soon," Naano says, before turning back to her audience.

Nana Abu shuffles back to the reception area and gets a folder full of information from Marissa. The gray-haired man has returned and starts to chat with him.

I take a seat next to Zayd on a couch by the door and start to play twenty questions with him. I've got a feeling we're going to be here for a while.

Chapter 19

There are at least a dozen white-and-red take-out boxes from Good Fortune sitting on the dining table, along with a stack of plates, a pile of napkins, and a jar filled with forks and chopsticks. It's buffet style, and we get to eat wherever we want, including in front of the TV.

"Help yourselves, everyone. Ami, please come and eat." Mama holds a plate out for Naano. "I'm sorry we didn't have time to cook for you. It's been a hectic week, and I'm completely exhausted."

"That's okay. This is much better," Naano says as she takes the plate, which makes Jamal Mamoo start to laugh so hard that he almost chokes on the egg roll he's eating.

"Ouch," he gasps between coughs, loud enough for all of us to hear. "Now, that's a burn."

"No, no, no, I don't mean it in a bad way, butthameez," Naano says, laughing. "I'm just saying that Chinese is a nice treat. This spicy garlic chicken is my favorite." She scoops some onto her plate.

Mama gives her younger brother a little punch on the shoulder.

"Ami likes my cooking just fine, right?" she asks. She doesn't wait for Naano to answer though and continues to speak instead. "Thank you and Abu so much for watching the kids all week long. It was a huge help for us and got us through a busy time. And I hope they weren't too much trouble."

"We weren't," Zayd declares.

"They were just the perfect amount of trouble," Naano says while Zayd nods his agreement and laughs.

When we got back home, after we finally left the Senior Center, Naano told Mama and Baba all about our field trip. She shared the names of the ladies she met, along with a shocking amount of detail about their lives, their kids' lives, and their pets. Then, after Jamal Mamoo arrived, she repeated everything to him again.

"Wait, so you went to the Senior Center for, like, half an hour, and you already made a bunch of besties?" Jamal Mamoo asks.

"Yes. Why are you surprised? I'm a friendly person," Naano says.

"Nice! What about you, Abu?" Jamal Mamoo asks.

"Well, I'm going to help make some improvements to the center," he says. "And build things for them."

"For real?" Jamal Mamoo looks at me for confirmation.

"Yeah," I say.

"Wow. You outdid yourself, Zara! Good job being camp counselor."

"Thanks, Mamoo," I say. "It was fun."

"You know," Nana Abu adds. "I was thinking that maybe

we can build one of the birdhouse libraries at the masjid, too."

Awesome!

There's no denying it: my grandfather has a real hobby now. As I watch him chat with Baba about his future projects, he already seems more like the retired person I thought he could be. I start a mental list of other things we can build together, like maybe a skateboard ramp for the kids on our street, a storage box for our outdoor toys, and, who knows, maybe even an extension to the clubhouse one day. We could use more space.

"Start small," Jamal Mamoo says, jarring me out of my thoughts.

"What? Did I say my list out loud?" I ask.

"No," he laughs. "But I can see your brain working. Think smaller."

"Fine," I say. What is something smaller . . . ?

"The marble roller coaster!" I yell.

"What?" Everyone looks at me.

"Naomi and I wanted to make a marble roller coaster during break," I explain. "Maybe you can help us, Nana Abu?"

"Sure," Nana Abu says. "If you tell me what that is."

I explain what a marble roller coaster is to my grandfather. And after listening to me, he gets excited about the possibilities and starts to talk about ramps and kinetic energy. It might end up being a Guinness World Record contender, the way his brain is working.

Apart from the marble roller coaster, Naomi and I still have the entire weekend to cram in everything else that's left on our list of things we wanted to do over spring break with our friends. With a little extra help, and maybe by convincing everyone that we should have later bedtimes, I know we can do it.

"I'm so glad you had a good time this week," Mama says, sitting next to me with her plate of food. She picks up some noodles with her chopsticks. "Even though you couldn't go to camp."

My mouth is full of fried rice, so I just nod.

"I love the way that you encouraged everyone to try new things, and made the best of it," she adds. "I'm really proud of you for caring so much about everyone being active and happy."

"Thanks, Mama," I say, and then take another bite.

Mama offers me a dumpling, but I don't have room on my plate and shake my head.

"I thought about it, and next time you have time off from school, I can send you to a day camp. There are some offered by the county at the community center that are quite reasonable. And a few of us were talking about starting a holiday camp at the mosque. Wouldn't that be great?" she continues.

"Sure," I say after I swallow. I glance over at my grandparents, who have already finished eating. Nana Abu is sitting on the sofa, dozing with a contented expression. Naano is trying to get Zayd to take a few more bites of the food and bribing him with dessert.

"We could also just go back for Camp Naano," I say. "Because I liked that a lot too."

Mama lights up and pulls me into a hug. "That's nice of you to say," she says. "Thank you, sweetie."

But I'm not just being nice. I really mean it.

"Amina's anxieties are entirely relatable, but it's her sweet-hearted nature that makes her such a winning protagonist."
—*Entertainment Weekly*

★"A universal story of self-acceptance and the acceptance of others."
—*School Library Journal*, starred review

★"Written as beautifully as Amina's voice surely is, this compassionate, timely novel is highly recommended."
—*Booklist*, starred review

★"Amina's middle school woes and the universal themes running through the book transcend culture, race, and religion."
—*Kirkus Reviews*, starred review

PRINT AND EBOOK EDITIONS AVAILABLE

SALAAM
READS

simonandschuster.com/kids

From the critically acclaimed author of *Amina's Voice* comes a slam dunk new chapter book series about a scrawny fourth grader with big-time hoop dreams . . . if he can just get on the court.

ayd Saleem, Chasing the Dream!

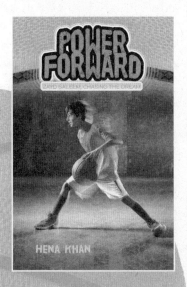

"Readers will cheer for Zayd."

—*Kirkus Reviews* on *Power Forward*

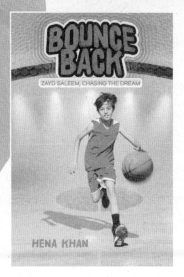